AF445312

WELL TO ETERNITY

flash fiction anthology

Ceeley Mack

ISBN: 9798668241170

"This Isn't So Bad" first published on everydayfiction.com in Feb 2018

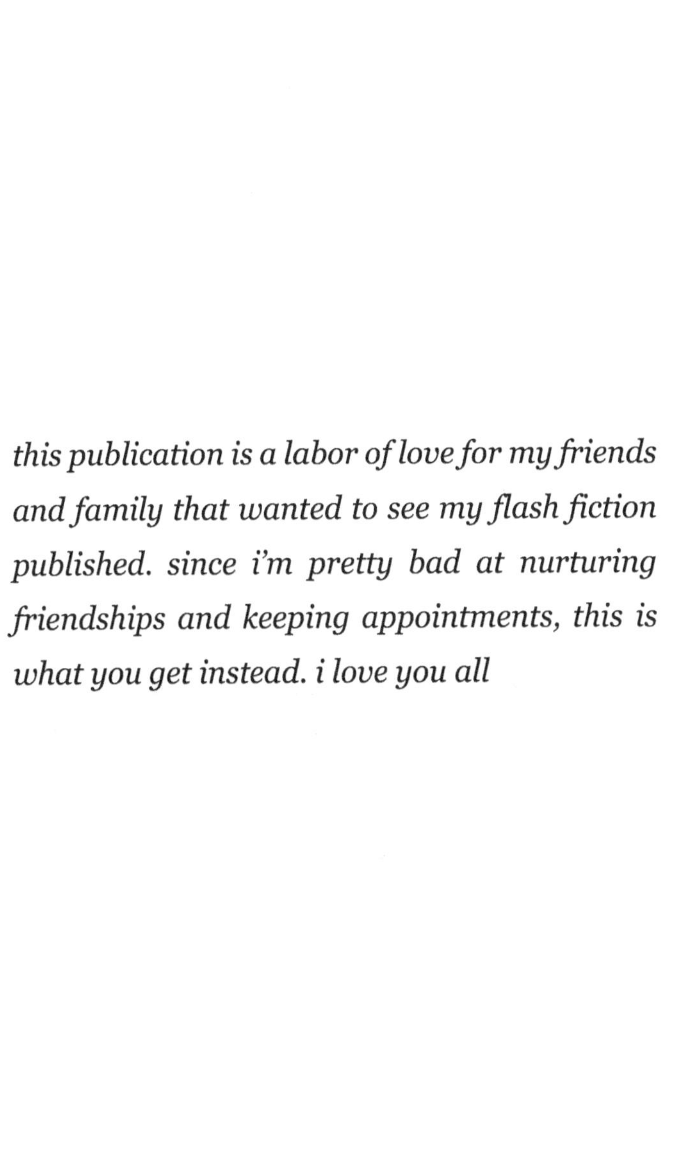

this publication is a labor of love for my friends and family that wanted to see my flash fiction published. since i'm pretty bad at nurturing friendships and keeping appointments, this is what you get instead. i love you all

CONTENTS

ON THE TITLE

Flashes come in pans, lights, and writing. They are only there for an instant and then gone, like driving past light posts in the rain. You look back, but you are already too far away. In flash fiction each story is a small window into worlds you quickly pass. There is no beginning and there is no end. There is just the impression that is left behind.

Each story can go on forever in a million different directions, and that ending is up to you. Your imagination is the Well to Eternity.

FOREWARD:
IN THE BEGINNING

I often wondered what story was the first ever told. Not a retelling of something that already happened, but real fiction. Did it start out as a big fish story that eventually became so outlandish that only the teller believed it? Did it start with a painting on a wall? Did the author know they were the beginning of a new art form?

My first story was a picture book called "All Dogs Snoop" written and illustrated by a five-year-old me. It included illustrations of dogs sniffing things around the house. At least one was a Dalmatian. It was the best a child could do, and my mother fawned over it. She kept that tiny book until I moved out of her house. She still might have it, I'm not sure. At the very least it began an obsession with writing stories.

My stories became a creative outlet and a sanctuary from a chaotic childhood. The characters and plots were one of the few things I could control and led me to spend more time in my writing than in the real world.

I had notebooks filled with stories, but any scrap of paper would do. (I still do this.) Even into my thirties I had a dozen notebooks with pieces of novels written in them. I've pared it down to one filing box.

These early stories were bad. Written bad, plotted bad, characterized bad. I'm glad most of them are lost. I go back and look at the few that remain. Train wrecks, every one of them.

But that didn't stop my obsession with writing and eventually the stories became better. I could think beyond my own daydreams and produce something that others would enjoy. It took way longer than I expected.

So here I give you a bevy of extremely short stories that were composed over the last four years. They are printed in the order that I published them on my Facebook page. They often reflected my feelings at the time of posting, whether funny or dark.

I hope you enjoy them.

FLASHER FICTION

Flash fiction is fiction often under five hundred words. I've collected my flash fiction into several word counts. Some are one-fifty, two-fifty, three-fifty and five hundred. The skill is completing a full story in an exact number of words. An example is this paragraph coming in at exactly fifty words.

-50

DOWN BY THE RIVER

I spotted him across the river. Just a guy in a suit with a large package wrapped in a bloody sheet. What a mess. It was like the man never disposed of a body in the river before. You need something stiff to make the body ridged, or you use plastic bags to hold all the messy parts. Amateur.

I dropped my carpet wrapped body on the bank and kicked the heaving weight into the river. It wasn't the first one. Sure wouldn't be the last. It wouldn't even be the last this week. Busy time of year.

I lifted my chin and stared at him over the reeds. "How's that fishing over there?"

He squealed and dropped the package in the dirt. Jeez, he had absolutely no idea what he was doing. "I didn't see anything!"

I gazed up at the sun. Sure enough, it was high and bright. Not a cloud in the sky. "Hmm, you should get a hat. Keep the sun out of your eyes."

The guy nodded and stared at me as he toed the package into the river. It plopped into the water and drifted lazily with the current. It wasn't even weighted.

He was going to get caught doing stupid shit like that. But I wasn't going to arrest him. It'd be a mite hypocritical at the moment.

"See ya around." I tipped my stetson and picked my way through the brush to my county truck.

"Yeah, I'll see you..." he said, "Sheriff."

-250

Notes:

This was my first flash fiction and inspired by a prompt from r/WritingPrompts on Reddit. It was also my first attempt at the twist ending. These short stories became a favorite mental exercise over the next couple years when I needed a break from school projects.

TEOTWAWKI

The world ended on a Monday. No one noticed. I spent that night in a drunken haze alone and miserable. I woke to a headache and hysterical screaming outside. I watched centaurs chase my neighbors down the street. The house across the road was on fire and a bevy of horned demons danced in the flames.

I went back to bed. Hangovers, man.

I didn't believe it was really the end until Thursday when my milk turned into snakes.

CEELEY MACK

I figured drunken bliss would be a nice way go out, but my neighbors thought the same. Every liquor cabinet, empty. I looked. Twice.

I sat on my porch and watched a crowd in white march down the street singing strange hymns. They weren't human. It soothed me to know other species were having an existential crisis too. Apocalypses should happen to everyone.

So, I drank my last beer and saluted the end. A white-robed creature left the throng and joined me.

"Want a drink?" I opened the cooler.

The beast nodded and took a soda pop.

"So, is the chanting and marching supposed to do something?"

"It's the harbinger of the end of times," he

Well to Eternity
rumbled.

I pointed to the melting sky. "We noticed."

The beast nodded.

"How long is this supposed to take?"

The beast huffed. "I'm not an expert in the death of all things."

I agreed. We drank into the night. We talked. We waited. Mostly we agreed that 'THE END' was taking a really long time.

-250

Notes:

This started out as the beginning of a book that I haven't written. I have a strange fascination with the apocalypse, especially when supernatural things are involved. No common meteors for me. I need demons or fairies or supernaturals of some sort. This will be the first of several references to the end of the world. Sorry.

ALWAYS EAT YOUR VEGETABLES

Billy never ate his vegetables. He just pushed them around his plate or fed them to the dog. One time at dinner, he stabbed a piece of broccoli on his fork and two tiny black eyes stared at him.

"Why do you want to eat me? I never did anything to you," the tiny broccoli said.

"Mom said you were good for me," Billy said.

"I'm just a poor broccoli. I can't do any

harm.”

“Okay, just this once.” Billy slipped the broccoli into his pocket and waited until after dinner to take the poor sad broccoli outside.

“Plant me in the dirt, behind the shed,” the broccoli said.

Billy dug a large hole for the vegetable and put the broccoli inside. “I’ll come back later.”

Soon his parents started whispering. They stared at him all the time. He didn't like it at all, so he spent time with the broccoli. It was growing bigger.

“You’re going to be bigger than me, soon,” Billy said.

“No, no,” the broccoli said. “Only as big as you.”

Billy stared at his plate and pushed the

radishes aside.

"Eat your vegetables. They're good for you," his father said.

Billy kicked his feet. "But they're just vegetables. What did they do to me?"

His mom clucked her tongue and ate the radishes from his plate. "It's important to eat all your vegetables. Very important."

Billy took a bag of mulch to the broccoli, but the broccoli wasn't there. There was a little boy that looked just like Billy.

"Broccoli?" Billy asked.

"No, I'm Billy. You're broccoli."

The other Billy shoved him into the hole in the ground. Billy yelled, but he was soon so tiny only squeaks came out.

"Don't worry, you'll like being broccoli," the

other Billy said.

Billy turned green and his hair turned into leaves. Soon the only thing left of Billy were two blinking eyes.

The other Billy walked into the house and hugged his new parents. His mom and dad worried and whispered, but they eventually stopped because he was a good little boy and ate all his vegetables.

-350

Notes:

I needed a story that children could read, so this one came from my daughter deciding vegetables were gross. This one has been used in a classroom to teach writing and storytelling, which I'm very excited about.

THE DOLL IN THE CORNER

Grandma sat a porcelain harlequin on my shelf. It had a key in the back that made it play music and twitch. I didn't like it one bit.

"I don't want it, Grandma."

"Don't reject a gift that keeps the monsters away."

"There's no monsters in my room!" I bellowed. I was too old to believe in monsters.

"Then it's already working."

So, the harlequin sat on the corner shelf and

CEELEY MACK

stared at me every night. Its eyes were alive and glittering in the reflection of the dresser mirror. Monsters didn't scare me, but dolls... dolls were creepy.

I stuck my tongue out at the harlequin reflected the mirror on my bureau, but my reflection didn't move. That was weird. Fear creeped up my spine. I pulled the covers over my head and peeked out.

The girl in the mirror was standing against the mirror! She looked right through me breathing fog on the back of the mirror. Mirrorgirl pressed her hands against the glass and slowly pushed out. I did believe in monsters, and this monster was me.

The harlequin's bells tinkled as it jerked. It was moving! Then, there was a gentle clinking.

For a second I thought it was Mirrorgirl scratching at the glass, but it was the doll clapping.

Mirrorgirl cringed and stared at me. "Molly, release me."

I shook my head.

The harlequin clapped and its music started to play.

My breath came short. They were going to kill me!

Mirrorgirl smiled with needle teeth.

I was paralyzed. The harlequin stood and jumped to the bureau. The harlequin clapped, and Mirrorgirl hissed. The doll clapped louder, and the music played faster. I extended my hands from the safety of my covers. It would not hurt me. I clapped once. Loud. Mirrorgirl hissed straight at me and ripped herself from the mirror disappearing into the reflected room.

The harlequin fell over on the bureau, and I pushed my covers away. I picked up the lonely harlequin and brought it to bed. If we were going to defeat the monsters, we were going to do it together.

-350

Notes:

This story combines two things that still give me anxiety, dolls and mirrors. A long time ago a neighbor collected porcelain dolls and one of those dolls was a white-faced harlequin with a key in the back that played music and moved. I hated it in the best way. Then, there is mirrors.

There is something about mirrors that are off-putting. I grew up with stories of ghosts in mirrors and evil things on the other side. Never trust a mirror.

SEVER THE SERVER

We shut down the final rack, pulled the plugs from the wall. The buzz of a dozen servers dwindled to silence.

Greg chewed his nails. "They'll start screaming soon."

"What?"

"Dead pages. They don't like dying."

The server room quivered and settled. Boss shut off the air conditioner.

"Do you hear it?"

I didn't.

"It's coming." Greg twitched and ran from the room.

He slammed the door. I was stuck. There was no handle on the inside. I pounded against the metal.

A popping plastic sound creeped from the back. I smelled burning rubber and sparked ozone. Something was on fire. I was going to die burning.

A voice sighed, a digital distorted sound. I scrambled backward and clawed at the door. Tendrils of smoke and tangling cords crept toward me. It was vile. Hands of blackened bone reached from the smoke and touched a rack. The servers screamed like voices of the damned.

I covered my ears trying to block out the

horror assaulting my mind. The darkness turned toward me and stared.

The darkness breathed in an electronic whine. I wanted to scream.

It reached for me with flesh charred fingers.

The door swung open, and the darkness collapsed, melting into the floor.

Boss leaned in. "No one in here alone!"

"Yep."

I scrambled up and ran out. The terror was fading fast, like it didn't happen. Maybe it didn't. We locked the dark building and ran to our cars. Even there I could smell the burning rubber.

-250

CEELEY MACK

Notes:

What happens when a server shuts down? Does all that information go away? It's the internet. It's supposed to live forever. What will that information do when it can't?

LOFT BED

My parents bought me a new bed. It was one of those pseudo bunk beds that you put a desk under to make it seem like the room had more space. It didn't.

It was great, but no one realized that the monster that lived under my bed now had room to stand up.

It reached over my mattress and scratched my back and caressed my hair. I didn't turn over. I never looked at my room unless I was safely ensconced in the light of the morning sun.

I just stared at the wall and prayed for morning.

- 100

Notes:

Rooms are small, and you might think that a loft bed with a desk below will solve all your problems. Well, it just makes new ones.

WHY I QUIT UBER

I drove for Uber once. Never again. I needed money. Some cash to make it through the month.

My first customer was this young woman in some old-timey white nightie. Some people have weird fashion sense. Not my business. She jumped in and wanted a ride to one of those dead-end *Deliverance* hollows.

She was quiet and intense. She didn't look right. Didn't feel right. I wondered about her feelings on murder. She didn't say shit the whole trip.

I pulled up a dirt road to an empty field. "You sure this is the place?"

"Yes." She wandered into the field, never looking back.

I was worried, so I followed. She didn't seem like the most all together person, and I didn't want to leave her alone.

Suddenly, the field came alive with lights and music. A party in full swing that hadn't been there before.

I didn't know what I was seeing. Dancing satyrs, Twirling fairies? An orgy of monsters?

My passenger returned and stared with big dark eyes. "Come with us."

I wasn't adventurous enough for this. "I have

Well to Eternity another pick-up."

I hauled ass out of there. I quit right then. Deleted the app and hid under my covers.

Sometimes, I see people waiting for a lift. They ain't human. They're going to a party. If I picked them up, I would have the time of my life.

But the day I do pick up one of them, will be the day I don't plan on coming back.

-250

Notes:

This is why ride sharing apps are bad. I know it. You know it. Don't get taken by the night!

SOMETIMES THEY COME BACK

He checked into the tiny hotel on the edge of his hometown. It was the only place he might be unnoticed but still within the forest boundaries.

The receptionist stared at him. Fifteen years changed people in a lot of ways. Some more noticeable than others. The receptionist was the same, only plumper.

The man sneered and tugged on his suit sleeves. He hated everyone that grew up in those small towns and never left. He had sacrificed everything to leave even once.

"Do I know you?" the woman asked.

His skin crawled. "No," he lied. "My room key?"

She slid it across the counter.

The man pushed a chair against the door to his room. No interruptions.

Chalk and paint made up the summoning circle. He chanted the incantation over the hum of the air conditioner.

A beast made of bone and broken flesh formed from the fog. Great antlers rose over his head nearly touching the ceiling.

"You again," said the deer-beast made of dripping dead.

He stood up meeting the beast head on. "You promised I'd escape this hell-hole."

The beast breathed deep, eye sockets lighting with fire. "You left. That you failed is your burden."

"You did this!"

"I don't intervene in my wishes. Humans fail all on their own. I promised you a way out. I did not promise you would never return."

"I can't be a failure," the man said. "I won't come back here to die in obscurity."

The beast raised a claw. "That is not my concern. Your sacrifice was accepted. Your wish was granted. Make another sacrifice to receive an additional wish."

The man stared at the beast. The receptionist was downstairs, alone. The woman had nothing to live for, a dead-end job in a dead-end town.

"I want another wish."

-300

Notes:

This story is the most personal to me and my struggles. It physically hurts to re-read this story because I don't know what I would do in this situation. What would you sacrifice to get out of the small town that held you down? Does doing whatever it takes make you a bad person?

BIRTH PLAN

I breathed through my fear as I laid back on the operating room table. The anesthetic was doing its job, and I couldn't feel anything below my face except a faint tugging around my midsection. Metal dropped on the floor with a clang.

I lifted my head to look at the curtain covering my open belly from view. "Doctor?"

"Uh, everything is fine. Just relax."

I stared up at the bright O.R. lights and

listened to the beat of my heart on the monitor.

The doctor cursed.

"What?" I asked. "Is it a boy or a girl?"

"It's... alive. Say, you didn't happen to make a pact with the devil and/or Cthulhu, did you?"

"Yog Sothoth. Why?"

"That explains the tentacles. Doesn't explain the horns. Congratulations, you have a world ending demi-god."

The doctor lowered the curtain, and I saw my precious baby apocalypse monster. "Awe, it's hideous."

-150

Notes:

This story came about when a friend had to

fill out a birth plan checklist and one of the listed items was "The ability to have a dialogue with my physician during surgery" which we all thought was a little strange, since the standard should be "get this baby out of me." This was the only reason to talk to a doctor during an emergency c-section.

.

HOSPITAL CORNERS, NEAT

"Make your bed, Johnny May," Mom said every morning. "You know what will happen if you don't."

So, I made my bed every morning. From the time I could talk until I laid my mother in the ground, tuck the sides, fluff the pillows.

The last thing she said was, "Don't leave the sheets out."

She was always so neat. I wasn't.

The day after she died, I got up from my

childhood bed. It was my house now, and for the first time in thirty-six years I left my covers at the end of the bed.

I didn't straighten it. I didn't tuck it in. I didn't fluff my pillows or place the final blanket over the foot of the bed.

No, I just threw the sheets back and left the room.

Nothing happened. Not the whole long day. I moped about and ate the food left by distant family. I sorted pictures and papers. Trash piled in hills all over the house as I went through a lifetime of junk.

Night came once again, and I trudged off to my tiny room at the back of the house. My blankets were askew, more than I left them. I paid it no mind, but the light flickered and glowed strangely.

None too thrilled, I touched my foot to the covers on the floor and pulled the blanket away from gap beneath. A gray wrinkled hand reached out and pulled the blankets back.

I should have made my bed.

-250

Notes:

This is my revenge for my days in the military and being forced to have hospital corners on my bed during basic and AIT. Just let the monsters take me!

SUN SHADE

We put up a sun shade on the porch. Well, my neighbor did. I bought the parts, but I was afraid of ladders and get sick even looking up. He brought his own hammer, but I supplied the drill. I don't know which one he used. By that evening it hardly mattered.

It's not like anyone watched the news anymore. They were too busy with Facebook and Reddit. We all missed the actual news of the meteorite. It was big. It was icy. It wanted a bite of the crust.

It's not like Bruce Willis could actually save us, and Ben Aflec laughed until he choked according to TMZ.

I stood on the porch and watched the sky darken as the meteorite got bigger in the sky. I was more than a little miffed that I spent seventy dollars on a sun shade that I'll never actually get to use.

-150

Notes:

This story is a product of our neighbor putting up a sunshade on our porch. That's literally it. And apocalypse love, of course. I lied about the meteors. I like meteors too.

NIGHTMARE CHILD

My first child is a nightmare. Not because she drops her cereal on the floor or screams when she's forced to bathe. No, she's a literal nightmare of flailing shadow tentacles and pulsating flesh. Essentially, pure joy.

The cat ran away the day we brought her home. Later we bought her a fish. At least it couldn't escape. But now its eyes are glowing, and it has started to grow claws. We would be concerned, but the fish said it was happy.

CEELEY MACK

Our darling gets along well with other children. It's the parents that cause the most problems. They are always screaming in abject terror when we come to the playground. People are so rude.

I swear they think their child is special or something. I know every parent thinks their child is the best, but deep down they have to know that my darling is going to be great.

-150

Notes:

This is not the same child as in Birth Plan. So, there are at least two monster babies out there making the jungle gym their lair.

THE HIVE

Grandpa open the top of the hive and held it up as I peek inside. The hive breathed up in a horrifyin' rhythm. Up and down, the drones crawled 'cross the wet surface, tending larva and honey cells. There was more honey than I ever saw before.

The hive hiccuped, spilling honey from the carefully capped hexagons. I covered my mouth with my hand. The hive called my name, sputtering wetly into the open air.

I looked away before I could vomit directly on the frames. I had to be polite. It was the rules.

Grandpa closed the hive and stomped toward me. He stared at me.

I shivered.

"Don't squall. It's just bees," Grandpa said.

"He was moving!"

"It was just the bees. Ain't nothin alive in there."

"Then why did you use my daddy for the hive?!" I screamed wildly.

He looked back at the man-sized box that held the hive. "Some things is more important. Sacrifice is needed. Bees keep the land alive. Your daddy... What did he do?"

I didn't answer, just felt sick. I thought my daddy done run-off when I was little. Momma said no different. If he ran, he didn't run too far.

-200

Notes:

I was in a pretty dark mood when I wrote this. My grandpa cared for bees, and I'd help. He'd hang the comb up in pantyhose to strain it into pots after it was harvested. It's a fond memory and commemorating it with a story about body-harvested honey is the greatest honor I can give it.

LOST BELOW

Skitter, skitter, scritch. Skitter, skitter, scritch, snap. I slithered between the spaces in the rock. I could feel the thousands of tons of stone that cradled me inside the mountain. It was warm.

The darkness was heavy and deep. It went on forever. It existed before me and would exist after. The weight of the mountain pressed against my ribs, and I flattened to squeeze through the gaps.

Fish splashed in the underground lakes. They were blind and cold living off their own decaying elders. I extended my claws into the clear pool. The fish felt the movement and drifted toward the ripples. Poor fools.

I dragged the wiggling fish into the cracks. Meat scrapped off bone as I dragged it further into the crevasse. I ate with wet sloppy slurps that echoed through the mountain all the way into the warm soft deep.

I lived in the abyss with air so stale even insects didn't venture there. In that lonely silent place, I heard a noise. It was a pushing, dragging noise. Moving between the rocks scrapping and clanging, I heard metal.

Sometimes they came here, creatures with metal and cloth. I watched them come and go.

Sometimes they stayed. Sometimes they screamed.

I found this one in the narrow crevasses far below. It wiggled and clawed, but it wasn't moving. It couldn't flatten itself between the stone.

"Help," it said.

I could hear its body swelling to further wedge it into the mountain. Its light had broken, the glass cutting its hands.

I whispered an apology and it screamed. The mountain moaned and the crevasse became infinitesimally smaller.

The creature groaned, its breath shallow.

I did not need the light to see this creature panicking in the dark. It knew its fate.

"Please," it moaned.

I licked tears from its poor flat face as I curled close for warmth. I could do nothing to help. This one belonged to the mountain now. I could only whisper the words of the mountain as it cried. My comfort would be accepted in the end. It had no choice. Poor fool.

-350

Notes:

My dad took me to Organ Cave and a few others in West Virginia and gave me a life long love of safe cave exploration. Interesting fact: the West Virginia caves were cold, the Texas caves were hot. Caves stay at the average temperature of the area all year around.

INFINITY

The captain had a headache before the ship went through warp, but orders were orders. It was risky taking the first human on board when the species was so new to the universe.

No one would be surprised if he didn't survive the first Voyage. There were bets on it. The Captain laid his credit on two weeks.

"Sir!" Second said as she removed her specially adapted visor. "It's Bradford. He didn't put on his anti-warp suit."

The captain laughed. "We broke the human already?"

She shook her head. "He's not insane. He's...fine."

***

The crew stared at the human sitting sheepishly on the med-bed.

"You were instructed to wear your anti-warp gear," Second admonished.

"Yeah, I tried, but It didn't really fit. I think I'm supposed to have tentacles," Bradford said.

"You saw the infinity of the stars with your bare eyes," the Captain said. No one survived seeing the warp intact.

"Yeah?"

The captain wiggled his antennae. "The infinity should drive you insane."

Bradford cocked his head. "You mean those moving stars should, like, make me insane? Geeze guys, you are out of your element."

"Explain," the captain snapped.

"I've been watching stuff like that since Windows 95."

-200

Notes:

This is another one from r/WritingPromps. Do you remember those Windows 95 screensavers? You could change the speed of the stars. It felt like you were floating forever. There was no end, only endless black and fading light.

FISHWIFE

The sun warmed the placid shores of the river. Sludge brown water swirled with bright green and yellow leaves, an aquatic garden of floating debris. I tended my own garden when I had the time. Otherwise, I sought out new specimens to fill out the rows.

I dallied on the shore with a childish delight. Young women alone on the river held a particular superstition.

A man in a vest and threadbare trousers sat

on the shore and threw his line into the water. Fishing in muddy water wouldn't catch anything alive.

I waded closer to the fisherman. "What are you doing, mister?"

The man looked up with jaundiced eyes and a gray streaked beard. He smelled more of whiskey than the bait sitting in the cooler beside him. "Finding a wife."

I gazed into the cloudy river. The leaves sank deeper in the water. "You're going to find fish."

"Fishwife," he grumbled.

"How's that work?" I crouched beside him and watched the line snag on an underwater log.

"I catch her, then she have to marry me." He stared at me with his yellow eyes and unhappy mouth.

"That's it? No riddles or anything?" I asked.

"Where you get those ideas? They ain't smart enough for riddles, but they do like gifts."

He grabbed my hair and pushed me under. I gasped allowing muddy water to rush into my lungs. Darkness screamed at the edge of my vision, and I succumbed to the river.

The man laughed and giggled at my death. "Here fishy, fishy," he whispered.

I opened my eyes and pushed myself out of the river. Oxygen hurt my lungs. Change was a painful process. Scales formed on my hands, claws on my fingertips. My eyes burned in the sunlight, ready for the dreary depths of the river bottom. "You found me."

The man stared at me in wide eyed terror, regret written across his face. He came here for me. I would leave with him. I grabbed his wrist and leapt into the river. He would have his wife.

I would have another for my garden.

-350

Notes:

I've rewritten this piece a dozen times. I've never been happy with it, and I never will be. I want too much out of it. So, I'll leave it as it is and let you judge. Also, river mermaids are not chill mermaids.

ONE TRUE FEAR

Pastel nuzzled her son's snout under in the dark and waited for the last lights to flicker out. Only a small night light continued to burn. The baby in the crib stirred, and the horde held their breath.

It settled, and Pastel breathed again.

"It's time," said one.

"It's time," said another.

Pastel pressed her hide against Powderpuff. He was too young for this, all legs and tail. Too young to go through the trials, too young to steal a baby's breath alone.

Powderpuff moved, his claws clicking on the hardwood. So loud. The baby would wake. If the lights came on it was the end. He'd be ashes.

She begged him to take the Trial of the Socks before he was saddled with full adulthood, but he wouldn't listen. Pastel lost three of her offspring to the light already and her own tail.

Powderpuff reached the crib and tugged the blankets between the bars. It was foolish to pull the covers. He reached higher, touched the top, pulled himself over. The crib creaked.

He wouldn't make it.

The baby gurgled then quieted. Powderpuff breathed in its breath. The baby gasped and gasped again. Its breath hiccuped then stopped.

Success!

-200

Notes:

I wrote this story when the kids were tiny. SIDS is scary and has affected my extended family. I wanted to turn it into something that could be battled, like a horde of lizard monsters instead of the invisible force it really is.

AND PEOPLE WHO TALK IN THE THEATER

I sat in the back row against the wall. I could see everything down to the first row. It was empty except for a couple toward the front. Some young idiot on a date with a girl too pretty for him.

The movie wasn't good. I pecked out a text on my phone, but the wife wasn't getting the gist. Texting is damn inconvenient.

"Claire, what do you want?" I snapped into the receiver.

The couple in the lower row glared at me. I tossed a handful of popcorn at them. Mind your own business.

The theater rumbled, and my call cut off. I scowled at my phone as the rest of the electricity cut out. The only sound in the room was the ticking of the film sliding through a projector reel.

The screen flickered to life bathing the theater in a strobe of white. Under the seats something moved in the flashing light. The creature crawled toward me bringing the stench of rotting popcorn. I tried to run, but I couldn't move. I was stuck to the floor. An emaciated hand extended from under the seats and grabbed my ankle in a sticky, cold grip.

"Shhhhhhhhhhhhhhhhh," the creature whispered.

I nodded.

The creature released me and slithered under the seats. The ambient lights returned and the movie flickered to life.

In a blink everything was normal, only the smell of burnt popcorn remained.

I breathed heavily and got up to leave. The boy looked back and smiled darkly.

-250

CEELEY MACK

Notes:

This story came when a friend told me about the electricity going out while in a theater. It was already eerie, so I made it worse.

SEAT YOURSELF

"Never seat anyone behind the rope," my trainer said. "That's just the way it is."

That was her answer to a lot of things in between popping her bubble gum and flirting with the bartender.

I did my best to be a good hostess. Always courteous and kind. I kept that perfect smile even when we were slammed and every customer wanted a piece of my hide.

Still, even on our worst days I didn't put anyone behind the rope, no matter how much a guest asked.

There weren't many guests that afternoon. Dinner rush hadn't hit, and the lunch bunch had cleared out. I took a quick trip to the kitchen to grab a roll, and came back a family waiting to be seated.

"There you are, we've been waiting forever. Get us a table," the mother said.

I plastered on a smile and brought her to a table.

"No, no. The sun is right in our eyes. We need to sit over there." She pointed to the roped-off corner.

"I can lower the curtains, Ma'am," I said. "We don't seat in that corner."

"Are my children not good enough for the shaded seats?" she huffed.

If possible, my smile got wider. "No ma'am. We don't use those tables. Wait one moment and I'll bring down the blinds."

I warned the servers about our *Code Karen,* and my poor trainer trudged from the back room.

I pointed her toward the table, but the family was gone. My trainer gasped, and sure enough they were behind the rope.

"I have to call the manager," she said.

The woman sneered at me, triumphant. Then, the floor began to glow. A huge circle and strange symbols rose from the floor. The woman stared in fear.

I stepped toward her, but with a pop they all disappeared. I put my hand on my mouth and stared. They were just gone.

My trainer walked back out and hung up the phone.

"The people, they just disappeared!" I said.

"Who?"

"The...the people behind the rope."

She laughed. "We don't put people behind the rope."

I returned to the hostess stand. No one ever remember why we roped off that corner of the restaurant. No one ever remember when someone suddenly stopped existing behind the rope. And if I seated a few bad guests behind the

Well to Eternity rope— it wasn't like anyone was going to remember.

-400

Notes:

My sister-in-law is a server. Though she has never complained directly to me, but I'm sure she's had a few customers that she'd like to disappear. Please don't be rude to people that make and serve you food. You know why.

BREAK

The last three stories are not flash fiction. They are longer works that defy shortening, but I am still very fond of. The longest one clocks in at 1,200~ words, so it still won't take up much of your time. They are not in any order except to end on something funnier than sad.

HOLLOW SHROUDS

I was excited when the schools closed, and everyone was sent home for an "extended vacation." Things were happening in the world.

Big things, Mom said, like that explained the sudden lockdown.

Mom didn't tell us much, but it was all over the news, the disappearances. Everyday thousands of people disappeared into thin air, but only if they were outside. Only if they didn't wear a mask.

Kids couldn't leave their houses. Playgrounds and swing-sets sat unused. It was exciting, for a moment. It was just my little sister and me most of the time, alone in our tiny house while Mom worked. She was "essential." No one cared that essential meant she might disappear.

Molly and I sat in the bedroom, playing electronics and sniffing at the crack in the window for a bit of fresh air. Two months was already too long.

Molly stared outside; her face smooshed against the glass. There wasn't much out there, neighboring houses, the sidewalk. Sometimes a person walked by on the way to work. Nothing exciting enough to actually watch.

"Jessa, there's a guy in the driveway," Molly said.

I put down my game and crawled to the window. There was a guy. He wore big square glasses and a mask, but everyone was wearing a mask these days.

"I think it's Uncle Charlie," I said.

"Who?" Molly asked.

"Mom's brother. You know, the weird one." She frowned.

I jumped off the bed and ran for the door.

"Wait, Jessa, put on a mask!"

I grabbed a mask from the pile Mom left by the door and snapped it behind my ears. I opened the door to a startled Charlie. "Hey! Uncle Charlie!"

"Don't move!" he yelled.

I stood as still as I could, only twitching my fingers on the doorknob.

Charlie cautiously looked around, then came up the stairs and shoved me inside. He closed the door and locked it.

He cleared his throat and breathed shallowly. "Where's your mom?" Charlie asked.

"She's in the bathroom," Molly said from the bedroom door.

I rolled my eyes. "He can see that she isn't here. She's at work."

He nodded and looked around the living room before tugging down his mask and pushing his glasses up his forehead. "Have you two been outside?"

"No, we haven't been out in weeks," I said.

"So, they don't know you're here."

"Who?" Molly asked.

"Listen, I can't stay long. They're following

me." He took a glasses case out of his pocket and handed it to me. "Give your mom this. She'll know what to do. Don't go outside without a mask. They follow your breath. Don't breathe too hard, and for God's sake cover your mouth when you cough."

I weighed the case in my hands. It was heavier than any of Molly's glasses.

"You're not going to stay?" I asked.

"It's not safe. I need to go. Remember what I told you." Charlie pulled his mask into place and slipped his glasses on. He was out the door before I could say goodbye, and the door slammed closed behind him.

Charlie was so weird.

I held up the glasses' case, and Molly snatched it from my hand.

"Hey! That's for Mom!"

Molly ran to the bedroom, and I chased after her. She climbed on her bed and opened the case. It was a pair of glasses, just like Charlie's.

"You shouldn't play with those," I said.

Molly shrugged. "No way. That was too weird."

Molly put them on over her glasses and looked out the window. Her entire face went from vibrant pink to bloodless pale in an instant.

"What?" I asked. "What!?"

Molly slid down the wall and shook her head. I grabbed the glasses from her face and put them on. Nothing looked different, maybe a little skewed. I looked out the window, and my stomach dropped.

There were things, shrouded beings floating in the air. Spindly fingers reached out from the hollow shroud and touched the air like a flailing spider.

"That's not real," I whispered.

Molly grabbed at my face, ripping the glasses away.

"Hey!" I yelled and grabbed the glasses.

"Give it," she said. "You don't know what you're doing."

"No! It's my turn!"

We both pulled on the glasses and with a horrible TINK they broke in half. Molly jumped up and looked out the window with her one lens. I moved slower, hopefully the glasses still worked with just one lens.

I held the lens in front of my eye, and there

they were. The hollow shrouds drifted along, following no pattern and no conscious thought.

We pressed our heads together, and Molly grabbed my trembling hand in hers. People walked on the sidewalk, masks on, heads down, oblivious to the creatures floating around them. A shroud would follow a masked walker for a scant distance before losing interest and floating away. It was like the hollow shrouds could only sense people's breathing.

A woman gasped as she dragged a cart of groceries after her. Her breath puffed through her thin mask. A shroud drifted toward her, touching her as she struggled.

I shook my head, and Molly covered my mouth. We watched silently as the shroud followed her down the street and out of sight.

I pushed Molly's hand off my face. "What are they?" I whispered.

Molly trembled. She was so smart. She was always the better student, the better daughter. She always knew everything. "I don't know."

A man jogged on the sidewalk, his mask around his neck. A shroud followed him slowly. It reached out a clawed hand for him, but the man ran too fast. It was getting closer and closer. This shroud wasn't like the one following the woman. This shroud wanted to capture him.

"Guy," I yelled. "Watch out!"

The jogger paused, turning toward our window, and the shroud swept him up, enclosing him in the folds of his cloak. The hollow shroud crumpled in on itself, turned a wispy grey, and seemed to shred itself into nothingness.

Molly made a muffled scream. "He's gone. He's gone. He disappeared!"

I dropped the lens on the bed and ducked below the window. "It took him. That thing, it took him!"

"What do we do?" Molly asked.

I played with my half of the broken glasses. "We'll wait for Mom. She'll know what to do."

Molly bit her lip, but she didn't have a better idea either. She would have told me how wrong I was, repeatedly.

We closed all the windows and pulled all the curtains together. I didn't want anybody or anything to see inside.

Molly turned on the news and curled up on the floor with her lens balanced behind her glasses.

"Today the count of the Missing has gone up to 300,368, an increase of only 1,477 from yesterday," the reporter said. "The governor has agreed to open remaining businesses, though schools will be closed for the rest of the year."

I turned off the television. "Stop it. It's not going to help."

She put down her lens. "I wanted to see if they showed up on camera."

"Did you?"

She shook her head.

Keys jingled at the door. Molly and I tensed. Mom walked in, exhausted, and dropped her purse before pushing her mask past her mouth.

"Hey girls, how was your day?"

Molly made a high-pitched noise and stared

at Mom in horror.

I took the lens out of my pocket and slowly put it up to my eye. Mom smiled quizzically, but behind her a dark shroud floated in our doorway.

"What?" Mom asked. "What's wrong?"

The hollow shroud reached for us.

Notes:

I wrote this near the beginning of the COVID19 pandemic. We didn't know how long it would last, and as of this printing we still don't. People I know have been sick. People I know have died. It's an invisible horror that will not know the true horror of until years from now. I need to put faces to the things that scare me, and I've put a face to one here.

TURN AROUND

Time checked his pocket watch. The single hand ticked across the face to the beat of his heart.

Death was late.

Time slipped the watch into his pocket. He was used to waiting.

He looked over the expanse of hot burning earth. The final dull red star lit the planet in perpetual twilight. A small boy crouched over a mud puddle carefully not touching the delicate ecosystem resisting death in the dirt.

Life was tenacious, even in the worst circumstances. Time only watched the struggle.

The Chaos rumbled weakly through the dirt. A purr took the place of a roar millennia ago. The Chaos was dying, like everything on the Plane. Only the Void grew stronger, howling from the impenetrable black.

"Thoughts, brother?"

Time turned to Death. She was always like that. She snuck up on a person.

Death had the same ageless quality as Time, unlike Life. Something of the forever lived in her, but she was as temporal as the rest. When there was nothing left to die, then she too wouldn't exist.

"You're late," Time said.

Death smiled. "People prefer it when I'm late."

Time's gaze drifted to the boy. "He's been here for hours."

Life glared at them with piercing eyes far older than his small body.

Time looked away.

Death chuckled. "Do you fear him?"

Time was eternal, nothing frightened him. "No, I worry."

Death gripped his arm. "Everything ends, brother."

"I don't."

She released him and looked away.

Life kicked up dust as he approached. "When life ceases Death becomes obsolete."

Time refused to look down. Life wouldn't be

the one to sway him, again. "Time moves forward."

Life scowled. "All life on the Plane is gone."

Time looked from the puddle then up at the endless black. Life was gone, and the Chaos was following.

The Void yawned. It was waiting.

Time gripped his watch. "What if I let it keep going?"

Life snarled. "We can't exist without our wards. Mine are gone. I will disappear and so will Death. Do you want to be alone again?"

Time glanced at Death. Endings never bothered her, nor did beginnings. He wondered if she would make a better guardian of the clock.

Life tugged at his sleeve. "I am ending! Hurry or you won't have anything left to save. She'll

Well to Eternity disappear too. Will you let her go just to spite me?"

Time cringed. He was weak, and Life was right. He couldn't let Death go. He could let time continue. He could let the Plane die and renew itself. Death would return, and so would Life, but they wouldn't be the same. They would be the guardians of a new universe with different lives and dreams. Only Time was a forever guardian. Only Time would remember what came before.

"I'm sorry," Time said.

Life slipped his hand into Death's.

The Void howled, a scream of pure rage. It knew what he was doing, and that it was wrong.

He held up the watch. The hand struck twelve. Time pressed the fob.

CEELEY MACK

The universe stopped.

Time shuddered in the nothingness, but even then he couldn't feel it. Life and Death were gone as were Light and Dark. Even the Chaos and the Void were silent. There was... nothing.

Time waited. Alone.

It could have been minutes or millennia. He waited for a word, a whisper, from something greater to guide him. Nothing came. Nothing ever came when the Plane paused.

He twisted the fob, pushing the hand back to the Beginning. It felt unnatural, wrong. Time pushed backward until stars flared to life then to dust. Until the universe pressed together into the Chaos.

He pressed the fob again, and the universe exploded. The Chaos screamed its anger as it

Well to Eternity rushed out to touch the Void.

Time couldn't help thinking he'd damned himself to keep a single memory alive.

Death stood beside him, staring out at the renewed war between the silence and the noise. Life disappeared, watching his creations begin again.

Time sighed. "Did I do the right thing?"

"It's not my place to say," Death said. "Your decisions are your own. I only bring the end."

Dust and matter swirled around them, all the tiny pieces of the universe joining and breaking. Something new burst into existence in front of him. He touched the material, let it flow around his fingers. "Do you know what happens after this?"

"To me? Yes. I get to rest. I don't know about

you, brother." She was so tired. Like it was all too much for Death to do again.

Time gasped pulling his hand away from the new element. "You wanted to end."

"I do." She said it calm and cold, the laying down of a burden.

"But Life..." he argued. Death wouldn't move on without Life. As much as Time hated him guardian, Death would always love Life.

Death smiled sadly. "Life will always try to live, even when I'm holding its hand."

Time stared at the swirling universe. He made a mistake. Again.

The Plane rumbled as the children of the Chaos and the Void came into existence again. Old guardians for an old universe. The guardians wailed, and Time checked his pocket

Well to Eternity watch. The single hand ticked across the face to the beat of his heart.

Notes:

This is one of my earlier longer works. I think it got up to 1,500 words, but I pared it down to a bit over 850. I learned a lot about writing since I first wrote about this trio. They are a part of a bigger universe that I have a basis for but have never had time to write. I hope to get that chance one day as I get better at my craft.

Anyway, this story came to me when I learned about the theory of the Big Bounce, as seen in Futurama. Though pretty much discredited, it's still my favorite theory. Here the universe is repeating, but it's a hobbled repeating, and we have to wonder what would happen to the universe in that environment.

CEELEY MACK

THIS ISN'T SO BAD

I died screaming. That happens when a three hundred-pound hellcat eats your face. But I woke up, so it was a little anticlimactic.

I always thought I'd be awed by what I saw on the other side. But, nah, the last couple years of apocalypse-level jackassery beat it out of me. Maybe Heaven would have changed my opinion, but this place, definitely not Heaven.

The landscape was a ruin of smoldering trees and blackened ground. Not a shit-ton different from Earth. The only big difference was the fire-red tint to the faraway sky. Earth was still a gray-blue horror.

The humming of a harmonica vibrated through the still air. It could have been the blues or hillbilly rock. I didn't keep up with either.

I strolled across the barren landscape. It didn't look like there was much to worry about. No people. No demons. All the demons were on Earth wreaking havoc and eating people's faces. The humans were... well, they weren't here.

I followed the music to a man in a fine suit sitting on a stump beside a fire. I didn't think it was cold enough for a fire, but I was a little out of my element.

But I knew that this guy, right here, sucked at the harmonica. Like really sucked.

I wasn't the type to just chill in misery. "Dude, could you not?"

The man stopped playing and glanced at me. His eyes smoldered like dying coals. Seeing the devil up close and personal might put the fear of God in you for a second, but I was pretty run around the bush by that point. Fear wasn't something I felt.

"You don't have to stay." The devil pointed a pale thin finger. "Door out is that way."

Lo-and-behold, there was a door ringed in blue fire and emitting a bright warming light. Something ethereal pulled me toward it, but I like to make bad decisions. I dug my feet in.

"Why are you still here then?" I asked.

He frowned and poked at the fire with an iron rod. "I can't leave. I'm here for eternity." He

CEELEY MACK

sighed, and the ground seemed to sigh with him. "They found a loophole. Too much torture. Too much anger. Too many lawyers. They found a way out. Everything left. The souls went to Heaven. The demons..."

"Went to Earth. Yeah, that kind of fucked us too." The world ended in an earthquake and an annoying amount of trumpeting. I was too busy drinking away my divorce those first few days to pay attention. Once my instinct for self-preservation kicked in the world was in shambles and demons were running the show. Though, if I knew I would be chillin' with the deposed king of Hell after my untimely death, I wouldn't have tried so hard.

The devil grimaced. "I noticed."

A scream cut through the still air. The devil

chuckled and pointed up. A small figure fell through the sky. I stared in abject horror as the figure got closer to the ground. It wasn't going to end well. The body hit the ground and splattered like a busted garbage bag. I wondered if I arrived the same way, screaming like a bitch and splattering like putty.

"Yikes," I said. It didn't even begin to cover it.

The devil with the deep coal eyes shrugged.

The mass of tissue muck crawled back together and solidified like a bowl of gelatin. Watching the whole process in reverse was somehow worse. I needed a drink.

The devil held up a flask, and I didn't even ask how he knew. It burned going down, and it burned in my stomach. I had a sneaking suspicion it was going to be even worse coming out.

It didn't take long for the mass to solidify and turn back into a fully formed man. The wholly solid man scrambled to his feet and looked around the desolate hellscape. I would have passed him the flask, that shit had to be traumatizing, but he took off toward the bright portal and threw himself through. Gotta say, he was a smarter man than I.

"That happen a lot?" It had to hurt the pride a bit. New friends show up and run off the second they get here.

"Every day. They usually don't fall from so high though. He must have been on a building."

"And you just sit here and watch them reform and leave?"

"Yep."

"Dude." I slumped down on the stump beside him. "You gotta stop torturing yourself. That can't be good for you."

He glared at me with flame sparked eyes. "We are in Hell."

"Yeah, but you don't gotta sulk." I gazed at the miles of crumbled nothing. "Don't you have a castle around here or something?"

The devil stood, towering over me with a supernatural air. He grew taller and larger into a great beast of a man with horns and claws on his hands. "I am the Prince of Darkness. Lord of the Flies. God of the Fire. And Most Feared in the Universe! I can create anything I need."

I had to admit I was impressed, but really, hellcat to the face ruined me for all the other monsters. "Well, right now, Prince, I'm your only subject. So, ya know, relax."

The devil deflated, literally, and looked around dejected. I couldn't blame the guy. After he'd run his very own hell house theme park for thousands of years, the tourists just weren't interested anymore.

"Come on, bro. Let's go to your castle, and I'll show you how to make a sandwich. You could probably use a hot cocoa too."

Satan sighed. "You are a strange soul. Alright. I don't have anything better to do."

I clapped him on the back. Hell wasn't going to be that bad. Comparatively. "Oh, yeah, toss the harmonica. The only instrument for post-apocalypse existential angst is a guitar."

Notes:

This was my first published piece. The premise came from a post on r/WritingPrompts, and I was able to workshop it in my Creative Writing class. It, of course, has to do with the apocalypse and survival, or non-survival. It's meant to be lighthearted. I'm sure they'll have a good time jamming out in the underground when everything above burns.

FINAL THOUGHTS

I hope you've enjoyed this collection as much as I've enjoyed writing it. I've spent at least four years on these, and in that time I've moved twice, got a bachelors, had another child, and published a book (not counting this one). These small stories show a passing of time and of the emotions that went with it. They hopefully show a maturation of writing, or, at least, of thought.

CEELEY MACK

If I can do all this in a few years, so can you.

Good luck to you, reader, in all the things you
want to accomplish, and remember, even the
small things count.

ABOUT THE AUTHOR

Ceeley Mack is originally from West Virginia and currently resides in Maryland with his family. He is an independent author of spooky fiction for reluctant readers. His stories are for people short on time or attention span.